STECK-VAUGHN
PAIR-IT BOOKS

One Farm

Written by Melissa Blackwell Burke
Illustrated by Laura Bryant

STECK-VAUGHN
ELEMENTARY · SECONDARY · ADULT · LIBRARY

A Harcourt Company

www.steck-vaughn.com

One farm

One barn

One nest

One hen

One egg

One crack

One chick!